For Jessica and Sasha

First published 1984 by
Walker Books Ltd,
184-192 Drummond Street,
London NW1 3HP

© 1984 Helen Oxenbury

First printed 1984
Printed and bound by
L.E.G.O., Vicenza, Italy

British Library Cataloguing in Publication Data
Oxenbury, Helen
The visitor. – (First picture books)
I. Title II. Series
823'.914[J] PZ7

ISBN 0-7445-0183-0

The Visitor

Helen Oxenbury

WALKER BOOKS
LONDON

Mum was expecting Mr Thorpney.
They were going to talk about work.
'You'll have to be good and amuse
yourself while he's here,' she said.

'Come in and sit down,' Mum said.
'I'll make you some coffee.'
'Will you remove the cat?' Mr Thorpney
asked. 'Cats make me sneeze.'

'Shouldn't you be at school?'
Mr Thorpney asked.
'I'm not big enough,' I said. 'How
long are you staying?'
Mum came in with the coffee.
'Mr Thorpney doesn't like our cat,' I said.

'Please put the cat out now,' Mum said.
'We must get on with our work.'

I let them talk for ages.
Then I turned on the radio and did
a bit of dancing.
'Please do that somewhere else,' Mum said.

I felt hot, so I opened the window.
'Oh no!' said Mum. 'You've let
the cat back in!'

Mr Thorpney sneezed.
'Look, Mum,' I said. 'Mr Thorpney
has spilled his coffee.'

'Oh dear,' said Mum, after Mr Thorpney had gone. 'He's forgotten his hat.'